James and Lucy Catchpole

You're SO Amazing!

Illustrated by Karen George

faber

Joe knew some amazing games.
So did his friend, Simone.

And their favourite
game was . . .

SEÑOR SHARKFACE PIRATE GRUDGE FIGHT

said a kid.

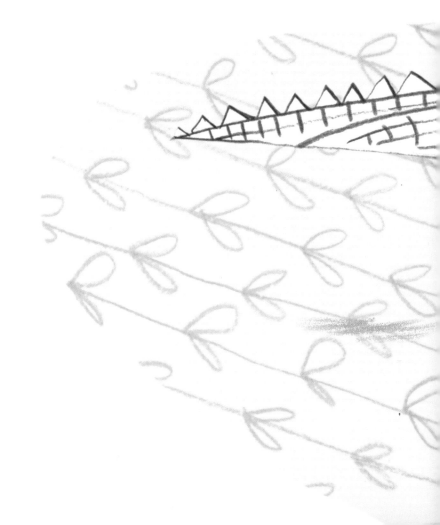

"I think she means
you," said Simone.

"Yup," said Joe.

And that was that.
Goodbye game.
Adiós, Señor Sharkface.

Joe was "amazing".
He knew he was amazing
because everyone kept
telling him he was amazing.

He was amazing when he slid down the slide
with Caspar and Ibrahim.

He was amazing when he hung on the monkey bars
with Yuto and Mainie and her sister, Viola.

Joe was even amazing when he was doing ordinary things,
like queuing for an ice cream . . .   or eating an ice cream . . .

. . . or just scratching his bottom.

"People need to relax," said Simone.
"I know!" said Joe.

Joe thought Simone
was pretty amazing.
Simone ran FAST
and jumped HIGH.

"Wow," said Joe.

"WOW!" said another kid.
"You're AMAZING!"
But he said it to Joe.

Simone was confused.
"But that was a REALLY
good jump! You were just
doing ordinary moving."

"I KNOW!" said Joe.

So Joe made a new game.
"I will make myself invisible and do some hiding.
Then everyone will say *you* are amazing."

Simone did her biggest jumps.
Everyone did their biggest jumps.

Joe just hid, invisibly.

"Poor kid," said a dad. "Do you wish you
could run around like the others?"
"I'm being invisible," said Joe.

"Sure you are," said the dad.
"But I bet you CAN run
  and jump, just like them."

So then Joe had to run and jump, because being Amazing Joe was better than being Poor Joe.

"Amazing!" said the dad.

This kid is SO AMAZING!

Sometimes, being Joe felt like being in The Joe Show.

And Joe didn't want to be
in The Joe Show.

So he found a game he
could play on his own,
without anyone watching.

When Yuto's big brother, Yui,
came past and said,
"Want to take some shots?"
Joe wasn't sure, but he nodded.

Joe's first shot wasn't great.
But Yui didn't shout "Amazing!"
He just rolled the ball back to Joe.

So Joe took
another shot.

Joe took A LOT
of shots.

And three of them actually
went in the goal . . .

"Amazing,"
thought Joe.

And that's how it was with people Joe knew, like Yui and Yuto, and Mainie and Viola, and Simone and Caspar and Ibrahim.

With them, Joe wasn't Amazing Joe,
and he wasn't Poor Joe.

He was just Joe.

This book belongs to:

....

This bc

The loa
a furthe

Faber has published children's books since 1929. T. S. Eliot's *Old Possum's Book of Practical Cats* and Ted Hughes' *The Iron Man* were amongst the first. Our catalogue at the time said that 'it is by reading such books that children learn the difference between the shoddy and the genuine'. We still believe in the power of reading to transform children's lives. All our books are chosen with the express intention of growing a love of reading, a thirst for knowledge and to cultivate empathy. We pride ourselves on responsible editing. Last but not least, we believe in kind and inclusive books in which all children feel represented and important.

First published in the UK in 2023, by Faber and Faber Limited, Bloomsbury House, 74–77 Great Russell Street, London WC1B 3DA.

Printed in India.

Text copyright © James Catchpole, 2023 and Lucy Catchpole, 2023.
Illustration copyright © Karen George, 2023.

The moral rights of James Catchpole and Lucy Catchpole and Karen George have been asserted.
A CIP record for this book is available from the British Library.

HB ISBN 978–0–571–37801–2
PB ISBN 978–0–571–37600–1

1 3 5 7 9 10 8 6 4 2

FSC
www.fsc.org
MIX
Paper from
responsible sources
FSC® C016779

For Mainie and Viola,
from Mummy and Daddy.
J. C. & L. C.

For Joe, Ivor and Arlen
K. G.